MM

THIS
BOOK
BELONGS
TO Tenisha Diane Brown

Disney's
SMALL WORLD LIBRARY

DONALD AND THE LOCH NESS MONSTER

An Adventure in Scotland

GROLIER ENTERPRISES INC.
DANBURY, CONNECTICUT

Printed in the United States of America.
Developed by The Walt Disney Company in conjunction with Nancy Hall, Inc.
ISBN: 0-7172-8223-6

Scrooge was delighted when he received a postcard from his cousins Hugh and Ian McDuck in Scotland.

"They want me to visit my bonnie homeland," Scrooge said, handing Donald the postcard from Loch Ness.

Donald thought the lush green hills and clear lakes looked wonderful. "I wish I could go, too," he said wistfully.

Scrooge began pushing buttons on his calculator. "Maybe you can . . . if you're willing to work," he said.

"I'll do anything!" Donald said.

"Good," Scrooge said. "I'll be needing a bellhop and a golf caddy—who won't be expecting any tips."

Donald was delighted. "Don't worry, Uncle Scrooge. Going to Scotland is enough of a tip for me!" he said.

LOCH NESS
URQUHART

After a whirlwind of travel arrangements and packing, Scrooge and Donald found themselves in Scotland on a dark and stormy night. As cousin Hugh drove them to Loch Ness, Donald peered past rain-streaked windows at the huge, dark lake.

"On a night like this it's easy to believe in old Nessie," said cousin Ian.

"Nessie?" Donald asked.

"The Loch Ness monster," explained Hugh. "It's a giant sea serpent many people believe lives right here in this lake."

"I didn't know there were monsters in Scotland," said Donald worriedly.

"You needn't be concerned with the Loch Ness monster," Scrooge said as Hugh parked the car in front of Castle McDuck. "You'll be too busy carrying my golf clubs to look for any sea serpents!"

Donald tossed and turned all night, dreaming of sea serpents. He was shocked out of bed the next morning by a loud wailing noise outside his window.

"What was that?" Donald shrieked, covering his ears.

"Ah, yes," Scrooge said dreamily. "I'd almost forgotten the traditional McDuck wake-up call!" Scrooge stood up and pulled Donald to the window.

Outside a lone piper playing the bagpipes marched across the rolling lawn.

"He's wearing a skirt!" Donald exclaimed.

"It's not a skirt, it's a kilt," Scrooge said as he got dressed. "A Scottish gentleman wears his kilt proudly—and so do his nephews who are traveling for free."

After breakfast Scrooge handed Donald his heavy golf bag.

"Now it's off to the golf course!" Scrooge said. "And you get to begin your work as a caddy right now."

Hugh and Ian joined them as they walked to the course.

"Did you know golf was invented in Scotland?" Hugh said. "It is said that a shepherd struck a round stone with his staff. When it rolled into a rabbit hole, he said to his flock, 'I wonder if I can do that again.' And that's how golf began."

Donald already knew everything he wanted to know about golf—the clubs were too heavy!

When they reached the first hole, Donald collapsed in exhaustion on the green. Scrooge took a ball and club from his bag and prepared to swing. "Stop panting, Donald," Scrooge complained. "You're ruining my concentration."

Donald held his breath. All was silent on the course except for the buzzing of bees. Scrooge bent his knees and drew back his club for a mighty swing.

Suddenly, Donald felt a bee inside his floppy wool tam-o'-shanter. Just as the club swung toward the ball, Donald screamed and threw off his tam. Scrooge swung wildly, and the ball soared off toward Loch Ness.

"You've spoiled my first shot," Scrooge scolded Donald. "Don't just stand there—go get the ball."

Donald took off after the white ball as it sailed through the air. He chased it down toward Loch Ness. But just as Donald was about to grab it, the ball rolled into the dark water of the lake.

“Where’s the ball?” Scrooge asked as he and his cousins caught up to Donald on the banks of Loch Ness.

“I can’t find it,” Donald said. “It rolled into the water.”

“What kind of a caddy are you? Go in and get it immediately!” Scrooge said. “Golf balls are expensive, you know.”

"The water is too cold," Donald argued.

"There's a wet suit back in the castle," Scrooge said. "Run back and get it, and I'll wait for you here," he added, sitting down against a rock.

Donald returned to the castle, grumbling all the way. "Some vacation. Wearing a kilt. Carrying golf bags. Freezing cold lakes."

When Donald returned to the group, he was wearing a wet suit.

He clapped the mask tightly over his face, then plunged into the cold lake. In the dark underwater world, Donald suddenly remembered the legend of the Loch Ness monster.

"What if there really is a giant sea serpent?" Donald wondered, looking over his shoulder. He swam straight into a tangle of weeds and branches, but he didn't see Scrooge's golf ball anywhere.

Donald swam back to the surface.

"Did you find it?" Scrooge asked.

Donald shook his weed-covered head.

"Keep trying," Scrooge said. "Swim out a little farther."

Donald nervously dove into the dark waters once more.

Donald swam far out into the huge lake. As Scrooge watched Donald's disappearing figure, he had a change of heart.

"Maybe I've been too hard on the lad," he said. "Perhaps I should just have him buy me another golf ball."

Scrooge wanted to tell Donald to stop searching for the golf ball, but Donald had disappeared beneath the shimmering surface of Loch Ness.

"I hope he hasn't gone out too far," Scrooge said to Hugh.

"You don't think the monster got him, do you?"
"Nessie's only a legend," Hugh said.
But Ian just shrugged. "No one knows that for sure," he said in a worried voice.

Donald searched the murky waters for the golf ball, but all he found was a lot of weeds.

"It's no use," he thought, kicking his way to the surface.

Donald looked around, confused. He had swum so far that he had reached another bank of Loch Ness, which was packed with vacationers. He stumbled onto shore and tried to remove the weeds and branches sticking to his wet suit and mask.

Suddenly one of the tourists screamed, "There he is! It's the monster!"

Donald looked around frantically for the giant sea serpent. But all the people were pointing at him!

Flashbulbs went off in Donald's startled face as people hurried to get a photograph of the monster.

"It's a little Loch Ness monster!" someone shouted from the crowd.

Donald tried to take off his mask to explain, but it was stuck tight with weeds.

The next thing Donald knew, a police officer was leading him gently by the arm. "This is no sea monster, folks," he said to the crowd. "Come along quietly, now."

Donald tried to explain what happened, but the police officer couldn't understand a word he said under his mask.

Back on the golf course, Scrooge was frantic.

"It's all my fault," he said. "I never should have sent Donald into the loch."

"Don't worry," Hugh said. "I'm sure there's a very good reason why Donald is missing—he probably got tired of looking for your golf ball and went looking for lunch."

"I'll buy him the finest kippered herrings in Scotland," moaned Scrooge, "if only I can find him."

Scrooge decided to go to the police station to get help. There he explained his problem to the officer at the desk.

"Bring out the sea monster," the officer said, chuckling.

Another police officer led Donald out of his cell.

"There you are, lad!" exclaimed Scrooge. "Got caught in some weeds, did you?" Scrooge embraced his soggy nephew. Everyone laughed when Donald explained the mix-up. Suddenly Scrooge had an idea.

The next day on the banks of Loch Ness, Scrooge, Donald, and the cousins set up a souvenir stand. Donald proudly posed in the weed-covered wet suit under a sign advertising "Loch Ness Monster Costume Kits."

It wasn't long before the booth was mobbed with tourists buying the souvenirs. Children eagerly put on their masks and chased each other around the loch.

"Playing monster is more fun than carrying golf clubs!" Donald declared. "This stand was a great idea."

"Aye," Scrooge said as he counted the profits. "And there's nothing more fun than counting cash—not even golf."

That night everyone danced at a traditional Scottish party, called a *ceilidh*. The sound of bagpipes, flutes, drums, and happy voices filled the merry hall. Bright kilts twirled in time to the happy music.

"Now what do you think of Scotland?" Scrooge asked Donald.

"It's a lot of fun!" Donald said. "I mean, it's a bonnie land. Thank you for bringing me on your trip."

"No, it's I who should thank you," Scrooge said, patting his nephew on the back. "Because of you, even on vacation I've managed to turn a profit!"

Did You Know...?

There are many different customs and places that make each country special. Do you remember some of the things below from the story?

Scotland has many large and beautiful lakes called *lochs* (LOCKS). Thousands of tourists visit them to fish, boat, or just enjoy the rugged landscape.

The Loch Ness Monster is a legendary sea serpent. The first reported sighting of this creature in Loch Ness took place more than a thousand years ago. Does "Nessie" really exist? So far, no one knows for certain.

The Highland bagpipe is the national musical instrument of Scotland. The player blows air through a wooden pipe into a leather bag held under the piper's arm. The player squeezes the bag with his arm and forces air through four other pipes. These pipes play different notes at the same time, giving the bagpipe a unique, rich sound.

Kilts (KILLTS) are knee-length skirts worn by some Scottish men. In northern Scotland's Highlands, each family, or clan, has its own special plaid design or *tartan* (TAR-tin) from which its kilts are made. The tartan design identifies the clan.

Scotland is famous for its lively folk dances. Young and old Scots in colorful costumes dance Scottish reels and Highland flings to bagpipe music.

Oatmeal is a favorite food in Scotland and is used in everything from porridge to a kind of flat bread called an oatcake.

Scotland has many old and fascinating castles. The most famous one is Edinburgh Castle, which sits high on a huge rock overlooking Scotland's capital city. It was once a mighty fort and is now a museum.

“Have a bonnie day, laddies and lassies!” means “Have a nice day, boys and girls!” in Scotland.

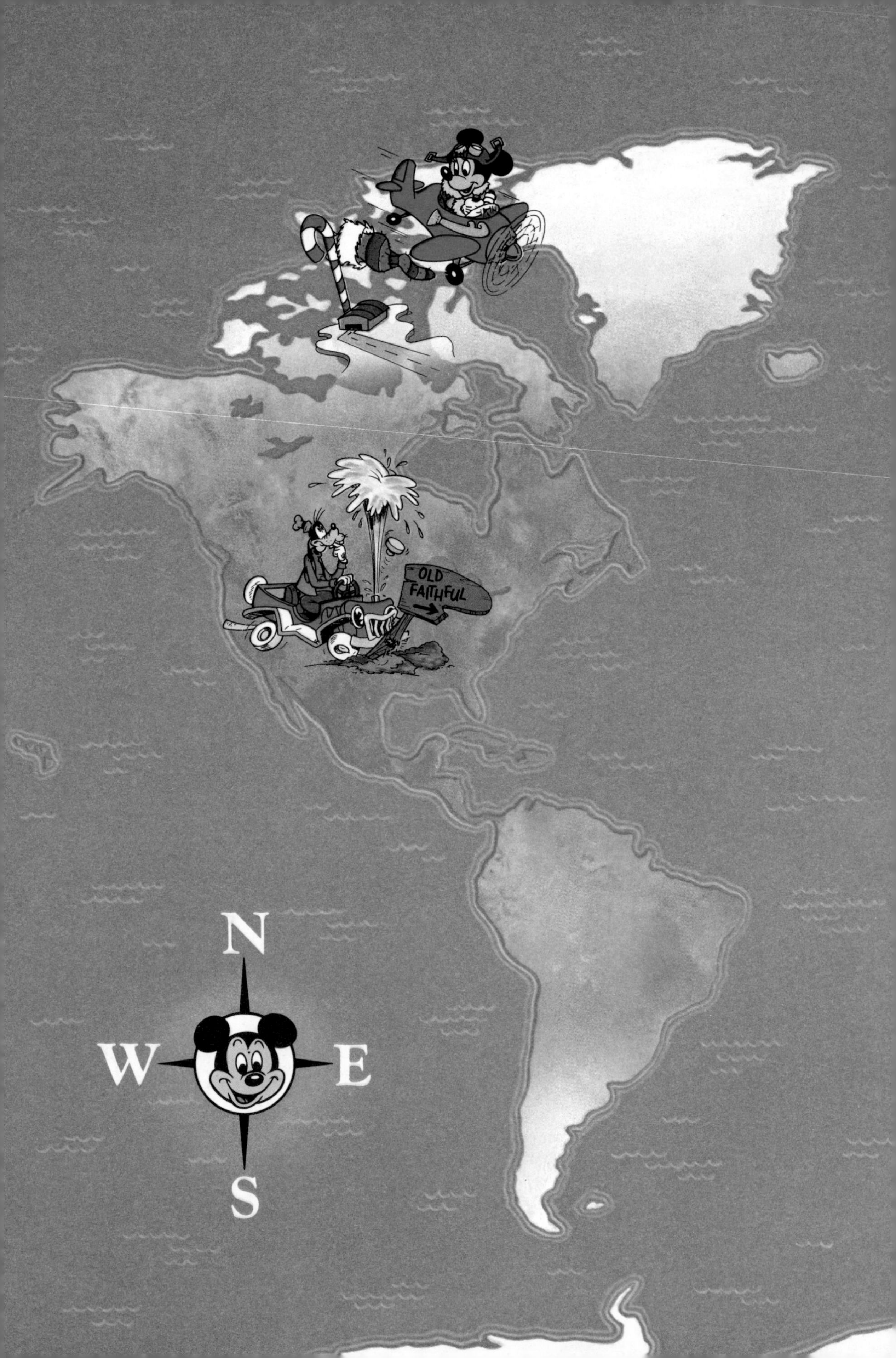
OLD
FAITHFUL
N
W
E
S